The Adventures of SUPER DIAPER BABY

Thats me!

THE FIRST GRAPHIC NOVEL
By George Beard and Harold Hutchins

THE BLUE SKY PRESS

An Imprint of Scholastic Inc. • New York

For my mom and Dad
— G.R.B.
To mom and Heidi
— H.M.H.

THE BLUE SKY PRESS

Copyright © 2002 by Dav Pilkey
All rights reserved.

Be sure to check out
Dav Pilkey's Extra-Crunchy Web Site O' Fun at
www.pilkey.com.

Library of Congress Control Number: 2001043899
ISBN 978-0-439-37605-1
26 25 24 23 22   18 19 20 21
Printed in the United States of America   23
First printing, March 2002

★ The ORIGIN OF ★ SuPer DiaPer BaBy

A introduction by George Beard and Harold Hutchins

Once upon a time there were two Cool kids named George and Harold.

were the Bomb!

me Too.

One time they were in the gym Running over ketchup packs on their Skatebords.

HA HA

HA HA

SPLASH SQUIRT

SQUIRT

It was fun until their mean Princ-iple, MR. Krupp came by.

HEY

CLEAN uP this Mess!

When Your done meet me in my OFFICE, bubs!

So they cleaned up the gym Floor....

SSSSS

...And went to mr. Krupps office.

You Boys are very iresponsible

Normally I'd would make You write sentences For a punishment.... but that doesnt teach You anything!

So instead I'm Going to make you write A 100 page essay on "Good Citizenship."

And I don't want you kids turning in a 100-page comic Book About "Captain Underpants" either! Thats is UN-Acceptible

Aw man

no Fair

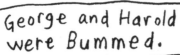
George and Harold were Bummed.

Why can't we make a comic Book About captain Underpants?

Yeah—He's A good citizen!

Then they got a great idea!

Hey, Let's make up a new super Hero And write A comic About him!

O.K.

So they went home and got to work.

The next day they turned in their 100-Page "essay"

What the---

Chapters

The Advenchers of ☆SUPER☆ DiAPer BABY

CHAPTER 1
"A Hero is Born"

10

11

But what Mr. and Mrs. Hoskins Dident know was that there new baby would have a Job...As A **SuperHero!**

DeLivery Room

weee

BuT... Before we can tell you that Story, we Have to tell you **This Story.**

This is Deputy Dangerous and Danger DOG. Deputy Dangerous is the one on the LeFt with the cowBoy Hat and the aposible thumbs. DangeR Dog is the one on the right with the Tail and the Flea problem.

RememBer That now.

EViL PLANS

To Secret LABratory

Deputy Dangerous was mean and Ruthless.

I'm am evil too

Danger Dog was also bad too.

I'm not really evil. I'm Just in it for The Kibbles.

Hey SHUT UP!

Together they opened up a Underware Laundry. But it was a TRAP!

YE OLd Underware CLEANers

underware cleaned while you wait

Super Heros Welcome

Soon came the moment that Deputy Dangerous was waiting for.

Tra-La-Laaaa!

YE OLd Under CLEAN

Look whose Hear! Its Captain Underpants!

My Hero!

then Deputy Dangerous zapped captain Underpants With His "SUPer
Power Taker-Awayer Ray 2000".

15

WARNING

THE FOLLOWING pages
Contains scenes showing
A baby beating up a
~~Bad~~ bad guy.
Get ready to be
OFFended.. ... Graphic
violins

22

FLIP·O·RAMA

HERE's HOW it WORKS!!!!

STEP 1
PLase your LeFt Hand inside the dotted Lines marked "LeFt HAND Here." Hold the Book open FLAT.

STEP 2
GRasp The Right-hand Page with YouR Right thumb and index Finger (inside the dotted Lines marked "Right ThumB Here").

STEP 3
Now Quickly FLip the Right-hand page back and FOURth until the Pitcher appears to Be Animated!

(for extra fun, try adding Your own Sound-Afecks)

23

FLIP-O-RAMA # 1

(pages 25 and 27)

Remember, flip <u>only</u> page 25.
while you are fliping, be shure
you can see the pitcher on
page 25 <u>And</u> the one on
page 27.

   IF you flip Quickly,
the two pitchers will
start to Look Like
<u>one</u> Animated pitcher.

Don't forget to
add your own
sound Affecks

Left Hand
Here

take this!

right
Thumb
Here

take this!

FLIP·O·RAMA #2

(pages **29** and **31**)

Remember, flip <u>only</u> page 29. while you are fliping, be shure you can see the pitcher on page 29 <u>And</u> the one on page 31.

If you flip quickly, the two pitchers will start to look like <u>one</u> Animated pitcher.

Don't forget to add your own Sound Affecks.

LeFt Hand Here

... And that!

29

Right
thumB
Here

... And that!

FLIP-O-RAMA #3

(pages **33** and **35.**)

Remember, Flip only page 33. While you are Fliping, be shure you can see the Pitcher on page 33 and ~~page~~ page 35.

IF you Flip Quickly, the two pitchers will start to Look Like yadda yadda yadda.

Dont forget to skip these pages without reading them.

Left Hand Here

... And some of these!

Right
Thumb
Here

...And some of these!

Ha-Ha. I hope Theres no hard feelings ABout my little spanking Acksident. Ha-ha.

HEY!

FLiP. ·O· RAMA #4

LeFt HaNd Here

ALL is Forgiven

RIGHT
THUMB
HERE

ALL is Forgiven

So Mr. and Mrs. Hoskins took there new Baby "Billy" home from the hospital.

SUPER DI-APER BABY

★ ★ ★ ★ ★ ★

Chapter 2
"The Evil Plan"

EVIL PLAN©

DANGER-CRIB 2000™

Deputy Dangerous and Danger Dog went straight to jail. But they exscaped.

CITY JAIL for Bad guys and dogs.

CRASH

I'm Free!

Hey!

Then they flew to a secret Labratory high on a mountain.

weeee!

SECRET LABRATORY

Now I will invent a invenchion to Get REVENGE!!!

Knock Yourself out!

So Deputy Dangerous worked all night on The Danger-CRIB 2000.™

that night

Good night, Billy.

Sleep good in your new crib.

Meanwhile back at the secret Lab...

Transfer Helmet

Haw Haw Haw! It's almost midnight. Soon I will be Transformed!

BUT

At 11:59 PM, something unexpeckted Happened.

MOMMA!

47

But at that very moment The Poop was Being Beamed to a satelite.

And Soon it was Beamed Back to earth...

...Right to Deputy Dangerouses Transfer helmet.

FLiP-O-RAMA #5

Left Hand Here

---Aw Maaaaan!!!

53

---Aw Maaaaan!!!

SUPER DiAPER ★BABY★

CHAPTER 3
Dial "R" For "Revenge."

When they got back to there Labratory, Deputy Dangerous began making a all-new invention.

Left Hand
Here

Who's Afraid of
the Big, Bad
Bug?

69

Right
Thumb
here

Who's Afraid of
the Big, Bad
Bug?

FLIP·O·RAMA #7

(pages 73 and 75.)

Remember, flip only page 73. while you are fliping, be shure to blah, blah, blah. You're not really reading this page, are you?

Well, since your here anyway, how about a gross joke? Q: What's the difference between boogers and broccoli?

A: Kids wont eat broccoli.

LeFt Hand Here

ALL Shook up!!!

Right
thumb
here

ALL Shook up!!!

FLIP-O-RAMA #8
(Pages **77** and **79**.)

Remember, FLip only page 77. You know, since nobody reads these pages, we figured they'd be a good place to insert subliminimal messages:

Think For yourself. Question Authority. Read banned books! Kids have the same constitutional rights as grown-ups!!!

Don't ForgeT to boycotT sTandardized testing!!!

LeFt Hand Here

Watch out, BiLLy!!!

Right Thumb Here

Watch out, Billy!!!

SUPER DiAPER BABY

★ ★ ★ ★ ★ ★

CHAPTER 4
" HOORAY FOR DiAPER DOG "

So Danger Dog flew Billy back to his parents house.

What if we make him wear a diaper?

Hmmm--- I guess that will be O.K.

And so Danger Dog changed his name to "Diaper Dog"...

Tee Hee

Doggy needs blankie.

Heres is a extra Blanket

... And a new crime fighting duo was born.

BUT ooo

Meanwhile at the New clear Power Plant, Something Terrible was Happening to Deputy Doo-Doo.

Don't call me that!

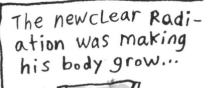

The newclear Radiation was making his body grow...

... and Grow...

... and grow...

... until suddenly...

I'm GonnA get You, Super Diaper Baby...
...and Your LittLe DOG too!

You know, I've seen PeoPLe steP on Poo Before, but I've never seen Poo steP on people!

Yeah, Life is Funny that way.

meanwhile at the Hoskinses House...

I will get Desert

Look up in the sky--- It's A Turd!

It's A Plane!

...No wait. You're Right... It's A turd.

And so with Lightning speed, our heros tied on their blankies.

And off they Flew.

"poopy - puncher"

Right
ThumB
here

"Poopy-Puncher"

FLIP-O-RAMA #10

Left Hand Here

Head Banger
Blues

97

Right thumb here

Head Banger
Blues

FLIP-O-
RAMA #11

Left Hand
Here

Around and Around
they went

Right
thumB
Here

Around and Around
they went

SUPER DIAPER BABY

★ ★ ★ ★ ★ ★ ★

CHAPTER 5
"Hapily Ever After"

On there way back our Heros stopped at mars for some refreshments.

man, these places are everywhere!

can I help you?

Yeah, ILL take a Large water... and a juice box for the kid.

me Like juice box.

New Alien Super-Power Juice

Gives you super powers!

Super Power Juice

will there be anything else, sir?

Hmmm

THE LAST FLIP-O-RAMA

Left Hand Here

And they all lived Hapily ever After

right thumb Here

And they all Lived
Hapily ever After

How 2 Draw
Super Diaper Baby

119

HOW 2 DRAW
DiAPER DOG

How 2 Draw
DePuty Doo-Doo

HOW 2 DRAW
THE Robo·AnT 2000

1

2

3

4

5

6

7

8

124

About the Author and Illustrator

GEORGE BEARD (age 9 3/4) is the co-creator of such wonderful comic book characters as Captain Underpants, Timmy the Talking Toilet, and The Amazing Cow Lady.

Besides making comics, George enjoys skateboarding, watching TV, playing video games, pulling pranks, and saving the world. His favorite food is chocolate chip cookies.

George lives with his mom and dad, and his two cats, Porky and Buckwheat. He is currently a fourth grader at Jerome Horwitz Elementary School in Piqua, Ohio.

HAROLD HUTCHINS (age 10) has co-written and illustrated more than 30 comic books with his best pal (and next-door neighbor), George Beard.

When he is not making comics, Harold can usually be found drawing or reading comics. He also enjoys skateboarding, playing video games, and watching Japanese monster movies. His favorite food is gum.

Harold lives with his mom and his little sister, Heidi. He has five goldfish named Moe, Larry, Curly, Dr. Howard, and "Superfang."

We're Sorry !!!

If you were offended by this book, Please send a self-addressed, stamped, businessed-sized envelope to:

Your name
and address

"Me was Offended
by Super Diaper Baby"
c/o Scholastic Inc.
P. O. Box 711
New York, NY 10013-0711

...And we'll send you more offensive stuff.